# MIRACULOUS PHRASES

## 7 Untold Phrases to Instant Peace and Happiness

## JAPJOT KANG

Clever Fox®
PUBLISHING

**Chennai • Bangalore**

CLEVER FOX PUBLISHING
Chennai, India

Published by CLEVER FOX PUBLISHING 2024
Copyright © Japjot Kang 2024

# Contents

# Acknowledgements

First of all I'd like to thank my parents and my brother for always believing in my ideas and my vision of making this world a better place to live in.

I'm grateful to Jatin Gupta for his presence in my life as a book-writing mentor. He is the reason why people are going through this sentence right now.

I owe a deep sense of gratitude to Graham Nicholls, Steven Burns, Ram Verma and Dr. Nitin Mohan Lal for equipping me with wonderful Neuro-Linguistic Programming skills.

My heartfelt thanks goes to the people who come across me regularly in my life for being open to my ideas, listening to them patiently and importantly sharing their valuable feedback.

I'm forever indebted to my college teachers, who never doubted my abilities and always instilled belief in me of doing great things in life.

(JAPJOT KANG)

# Introduction

The world is progressing at a fast pace. Our phones for instance aren't similar to those in the 2000's. The speed with which we do things is much faster, the technology is progressing and the science of the mind has progressed, so instead of being stuck for a long time in a negative emotion and spending hours and days to get rid of it, we can get rid of it in minutes. One doesn't have to be a prisoner to their negative emotions when one can be an emperor instead. That's where this book comes in. Welcome to my world of mental wellness where life is a rising sun. Making changes in ourselves is simple yet effective. One can overcome different scars from their lives and the only requirement is that one is willing to change what's not working for them and pursue something useful that'll work wonders for them. That something useful for us would be instant peace and happiness right now. The information in this book is first applied to me and others and only then presented to you so you can be rest assured that you are in for a treat. So let's embark on this wonderful journey together.

## CHAPTER 1

# THE CURRENCY OF YOUR LIFE

## What exactly is the currency of life?

The currency of life is how one spends the moments of their day. One plans to be negative and think about what is lacking and going wrong in their life 2 minutes here, 5 minutes there and another 10 minutes there and it adds up to 60 minutes a day, that's 30 hours a month, 365 hours a year and 3650 hours in 10 years. So one is adequately planning against oneself to lose all that valuable time. Just think about it, wouldn't it be great if one does something valuable with all that time? I'm sure it would be.

Just imagine for a couple of seconds, how good it would be to learn the skill of successfully planning what you'd like to experience more of. This book will empower us with simple yet effective steps to make the most out of the 1440 minutes we all have in a day and achieve more of what we want in our life and that's peace and happiness for us.

**Q. How would you like to primarily like to spend the moments of your day?**

-

# CHAPTER 2

# CHILD-LIKE MENTALITY

*T*he best mentality to possess while reading this book is a child-like one. Remember that good old time when we as a child wanted to become something one day and something else the other and we never questioned how it would happen or thought about if it was even possible or never asked ourselves whether we were good enough, worthy enough to accomplish that very thing in life. We were so open to new ideas, and we'd let our imaginations float freely. I'm sure we were able to get in touch with the younger version of ourselves and access that golden time of our lives.

I'll request all of us to be open to implementing the different ideas we'll learn from this book and listen to the inner us, who would want nothing but the absolute best for us. And we'd individually call it the "inner me". In the same way, you never questioned your Math teacher at school when they wanted you to suppose if X = something, Y = something, what would be The value of XY or how would learning something particular help us in our lives? We just accepted the ideas and went ahead with it.

In the same way, I would like you to further progress with this book and experience how everything fits in. To get in the absolute right mindset, I would like to share my favourite quote with you –

*"Whether you think you can or you think you can't, you're right."*

**HENRY FORD**

**Q. Were you able to access the inner child in you and that golden time when you fully believed in yourself?**

# CHAPTER 3

# WORDS AND OUR 5 SENSES

Our words have energy and they have the power to shape our reality. The words we use daily impact our day-to-day experiences in life. Every word we say creates a relevant image in our mind. Just try reading these words one at a time and notice the image that is being created in your mind.

## Dog Chocolate Door Mirror

Now the images you make could be real-life ones or they could be animated, but the major takeaway from this little exercise was to show you the relationship between words and images we make. This process happens automatically whether one is aware of it or not. There are 2 types of words primarily which we will learn about later in the book - the high-energy words and the low-energy words. All of these words create relevant images in our minds.

It is something we do automatically and this is how we process words in our mind.

These words create more than just images and that is what we're going to learn about next. Let me introduce you to a relatively new term but a very useful one, Sub-modalities.

Sub-modalities simply refer to the quality of our senses.

We experience our world through 5 senses namely visual (sight), auditory (hearing), kinesthetic (internal and external feelings), olfactory (smell) and gustatory (taste). Our primary ones are the visual, auditory and kinesthetic ones and let's call them see, hear and feel for now.

Now is the time for a quick exercise. Do chant focus, focus, and focus a couple of times before you start the exercise. First, close your eyes and tell your name to yourself - my name is ...... (Repeat it 5 times) and then tell yourself a name that isn't your name – My name is XYZ (Repeat it 5 times) and just notice what you see, hear and your feelings about it. The first line with your real name would sound and feel confident and true when compared to the second line that isn't your name as that sounds and feels false and has doubt in it. There would be a major difference in the location of both the images as well as one could be in one direction and the other in another. You can repeat the exercise once more to get a good hang of it.

Another quick example of this would be to say yourself internally a true statement and a false statement like repeating the following statement 5 times - The sun rises in the east and notice what its image and sound are like, and notice the feelings that arise from the true statement. On the contrary, I'd suggest you to repeat the following statement 5 times - The sun rises in the south and now what the image, sound and feelings are like.

Does it sound true, feel right or the image is as clear as the true statement? Please do this quick exercise as it will act as a building block for something we would like to do in the last chapter of the book.

This book involves playing around with your sub-modalities like what you see, hear and feel and being good at this skill will enable you to magnify pleasant experiences and weaken the unpleasant ones later in the book. This is the most important skill that will be required to get the best out of this book and you'll get the why behind the last chapter of the book. And how to use this skill to create moments of instant peace and happiness in our lives. Just imagine for a couple of seconds, how good it would be.

**Q. Are you fully aware of what are Sub-modalities and our 3 primary senses? (yes, no or maybe) If it's a no or a maybe, please go through it once again before you proceed with the next chapter.**

# CHAPTER 4

# WHAT ARE WE TELLING OURSELVES?

We all come into this world as a blank slate and then soon, we're given an identity in terms of our name. This becomes one of the initial parts of our self-identity but if we see it like this, it's not our own, it's given to us by our parents or someone else in the family probably.

As we were unaware of who we were at the time of birth and we were unaware of the fact that life is a wonderful gift and we got to make the most out of it but now I'm bringing it to your awareness. Instead the world chips in and tells us who we are, what we can and can't do, what we're good at and what we're not good at and all this becomes a part of our identity usually by the age of 7 and it continues even after that.

Our Self-Identity is reflected in the words we use all day long. It has already pre-decided our limits and potential and we comply with it and we regularly say things like

- I am this or have been like this forever. and can't do anything about it. But I'm going to share some exciting news with you, You can certainly do something about it and shift your self-image. The only requirement is to know and trust the fact that you can and you will.

Now is the time to introduce you to the first phrase of the book that universally applies to all of us -

## SO BE IT

SO BE IT is used to express agreement or resignation towards something.

If you use such low-energy phrases like I am fat, I am unworthy, I am shy, I am not smart enough, I am not good enough, I can't, It's hard, guess what - SO BE IT. It'll be true for you and always has been true for you.

On the contrary, If you use high-energy words like I am worthy, I am healthy, I am good enough, Things are working for me, It's easy, guess what - SO BE IT. It'll be true for you and always has been true for you.

To make it easier to grasp, we can phrase it like we get what we ask for and it has always been the case for everyone. It's a phrase that applies to everything we believe in and if we have constantly received a repeated command of "you are this" or "you are that" from our family, relatives, friends, teachers or others, then after some time we start to believe it and it reflects in our self-image as it stands true for us as it's coming from a known source until we intentionally try to do something about it.

That was all right until now as we're going to change it for good through the quick yet effective follow-along exercises in the book. Just remember this fact for now, our self-talk in terms of all the limiting stuff we've heard was being planted in our head and we were not born with it. The only mistake we all make as humans is that we agree upon things easily and we think if the people around us are saying it, it would be true. I'd like to share my first quote as I think it'll be relatable at this very moment.

> ***"Whether you consider something to be true
> or not to be true for you is up to you."***

Until and unless it's a universal truth like H2o stands for water worldwide, we have the choice to choose what's hard, easy or impossible for us. I'm sure we all could relate with the quote. So now that we are aware of the fact where the majority of our self-talk comes from.

Always remember these and make these a part of our self-talk preferably before going to sleep or right after we wake up as these are the times when our mind is highly suggestible or at any time we find suitable because within a couple of weeks, we'll start to feel them as true and we'll be able to feel the shifts in our emotions.

The next thing I'd like to share are a couple of powerful phrases to shift things for us - I am blessed, I am worthy, I am whole, I am lucky or such empowering I am statements.

Because once we do, we will start to become it and if we constantly repeat we're not we won't be. "You reap what you sow" and if we are sowing potatoes and expecting carrots out of it, how would that work?

And now is the time for me to introduce the next 2 phrases-

## CANCEL, CANCEL, CANCEL
## THAT'S FALSE

Whenever someone says something that we won't like to be a part of our identity then use the words cancel, cancel, cancel internally or say that's false internally to train our mind to see it as a false statement and replace it with a new one - something we'd like to be and say something wonderful to ourselves instead. Just quickly think about a thing or two that's part of your self-talk and say them intentionally in your mind, practice the above 2 phrases after it and notice how your feelings change. Try practising it intentionally 5-7 times or more to get good at it. Here, I'd like to share my second quote, which will be very relevant at this moment.

### *"Brainwash yourself, the world has already done its part."*

We've always learned something in life and made things automatic for us, we have learnt to use our fork with the same hand, we've learnt to navigate our way to work automatically and we don't question which hand to use while using a fork or which way to turn as we go to work, same is the case for our words. To be good at something, we all learn new things through repetition and the sane stands true for our words.

I'm sure we all have empowered ourselves with the fact that we can change our words and changing our words, changes our energy and it changes how we act and what we can do.

In a nutshell, we should remember to tell ourselves what we want to be part of our reality and stay away from the things that we don't want as we're new to all this and when we do say something to ourselves that we don't like, use the phrases mentioned above or a combination of both and say what we'd like to have instead. At first, we have to be more intentional about it and then within a week or two, our mind will learn to make it automatic for us and give us more of what we want and less of what we don't.

Q. Have you completed the easy exercises discussed in the chapter?

Q. Do you promise yourself to brainwash yourself from now on?

# CHAPTER 5

# WHAT ARE WE TELLING OTHERS?

Our self-talk is directly reflected in what we tell others. One can't think about negative stuff all day long and talk about positive things with others. Of course, one can lie or pretend and all but for how long? What we say out in the world daily emanates a similar level of energy and if one is telling someone that I am doing this and it's hard, they can't do that, the exam preparation is hard or that particular subject is tough, is imposing their limitations on others. Because regardless of what we say and if the other person trusts us to some degree, guess what is being applied - SO BE IT. (knowingly for us now and unknowingly for them)

Our words impact others and can over time show up in the lives of others, yes they are this powerful. So we have to use our words carefully and more intentionally as they are creating images in the minds of others according to the words we're using in the conversation. So basically we are taking away from our peace and happiness and from that of others.

Now if the opposite happens, we're listening to someone and that's costing us peace and happiness, I'll share a remedy for the same in the next chapter. I don't want us to monitor every single word we say but just pay close attention to a constant area of problem like at work, health or relationships and then monitor our words around it and check how we can better use our words both internally and externally.

For example, if one wants others to feel motivated around them, then they have to be in high spirits themselves first to emanate similar energy out there.

A quick exercise, just think of a time when you thanked someone for something random or go and thank someone for something random and see how their energy shifts immediately.

I'll suggest all of us to remember SO BE IT applies to our external conversations as well and our energy is easily transferrable to others.

Q. Do you plan to closely monitor your words around a problematic area for you and observe what you're telling and is it emanating the kind of energy you'd like them to feel when they're around you?

# CHAPTER 6

# WHAT OTHERS ARE TELLING YOU?

$\mathcal{T}$he words of others carry the same level of energy as ours. They possess the same power to shift our views and perspectives about something and how we view our day-to-day lives whether knowingly or not. And we've discussed how the words of others have been doing that already and we choose to brainwash ourselves from now onwards.

Next, I'd like to share the 3 broad categories of people around us and see how they fit into our lives -

## THE WELL-WISHERS

These are the type of people who believe in some of our abilities and not in others. For instance, they may say go for it we can do it and in the next moment, they may doubt us and ask us are you sure?

Their words will guide us about the positives and the negatives of different things. Their communication will include a good mix of high-energy and low-energy words. They see the good and the bad in different situations of life. They are called well-wishers as they care about us to a great extent and want us to do good in different aspects of our lives. These could include our parents, siblings, friends, work colleagues, teachers or someone else. Usually, these types of people should be the majority in our lives.

## THE ENERGY SUCKERS

As the name suggests, these are the kind of people who love to blame and complain about things, find what's not right about them and impose their limitations and insecurities on others or constantly look around and see what not's right about others. They constantly tell and enjoy telling others they can't, that's not possible and all. They primarily use low-energy words and are very easy to spot. These could be a relative in the family, friend or a teacher. Be very careful, if the number of energy suckers is over the number of well-wishers in your life, you got to do something about it.

Now, let's talk about the third and the rarest category of people -

# THE ENERGY BOOSTERS

They are called energy boosters for a reason. They possess a positive attitude and have high energy. They manage to look at the positives in different situations of life. They hope and believe in the good of others and themselves. They choose and always appreciate things in life rather than complaining about things. They are so rare that one would come across a few such individuals in their respective lives. Now again, it could be anyone in your family, a teacher who inspires you to take that next step or it could be someone else.

Now, I'd like to introduce you to the next 2 phrases -

## NOT FOR ME
## BLAH, BLAH, BLAH

When we catch someone saying something we don't want to comply with, use the phrase NOT FOR ME in our mind so that the particular thing stands true for the particular person saying it and not for us. We can nod our heads but know that the phrase we tell ourselves internally is stronger than any suggestion coming our way. Using this phrase will help us to shield and protect ourselves from others limiting ideas and when we start using it intentionally, it will soon become automatic for us in two to three weeks and we will find our mind automatically negates the stuff it doesn't want.

And if we find someone who's affecting our energy and costing us peace and happiness, don't hesitate to use the above phrase or try saying BLAH, BLAH, BLAH internally but a serious one this time to let our mind know that we don't care about the thing that's coming our way. We can also cross our fingers or legs signifying we're being protected at that time. Now BLAH, BLAH, BLAH would be a familiar casual phrase for all of us but we mean it from now on. Mix and match all these things and see what works best for you.

**Q. Which category out of the 3 do you belong in primarily when showing up in the lives of others?**

# LET'S REVIEW

We're beyond the halfway mark of this book. There are 3 major takeaways we have to progress with and get hold of.

- **Our words have energy**
- **The 3 different types of talks**
- **The 3 broad categories of people in our lives**

# LIST OF HIGH-ENERGY AND LOW-ENERGY WORDS

| | |
|---|---|
| Energy | Lazy |
| Enthusiasm | Envy |
| Good | Bad |
| Harmony | Hard |
| Thanks | Worry |
| Happy | Anxiety |
| Improve | Angry |
| Free | Afraid |
| Feeling | Worse |
| Family | Doubt |
| Achieve | Hard |
| Unique | Weak |
| Positively | Mean |

| | |
|---|---|
| Certainly | Guilt |
| Absolutely | Stupid |
| Definitely | Trying |
| Obviously | Difficult |
| Choose or choice | Rage |

# SWITCH YOUR OR OTHER'S ENERGY IMMEDIATELY

Fact - Our mind doesn't process words like not, don't as we think we do. If I say right now please don't think about a pink elephant or the colour of the walls in your bedroom. What you just did was do something even though you were asked not to do it, so just say what you want and not what you don't want. For example, notice the difference between the two, don't drop the ball and catch the ball. What images would both the commands create in your mind.

## A LIST OF WORDS TO SWITCH YOUR OR SOMEONE ELSE'S ENERGY

That's not bad - That's quite good

No problem - You're very welcome

That's bad - That's not good

Don't worry - You'll be fine

Put some effort into it - Put some energy into it

It's too hard - It's not easy

I'm sick - I don't feel well

I've been working hard - I've been working well

No problem - You're very welcome

Diet plan - Nourishment plan

I was bad today - I didn't do very well today

Fat - Not slim

I'm feeling down - I'm clearing some emotions right now

Use the trigger word "Change" whenever you catch yourself using a low-energy dialogue. These are subtle changes that we can use to create better images in our minds and feel good about them.

Now we don't have to monitor every word we say, all we have to look for a certain problematic area in our lives and use the 3-step OCC framework to improve the particular area of our lives.

- **Observe it**
- **Catch it**
- **Change it**

# THE MOOD LOOP

We're clear with how words pre-define the kind of experiences we have in our lives. I would like to share 5 important concepts to further solidify our belief in words and phrases to achieve instant peace and happiness in our lives.

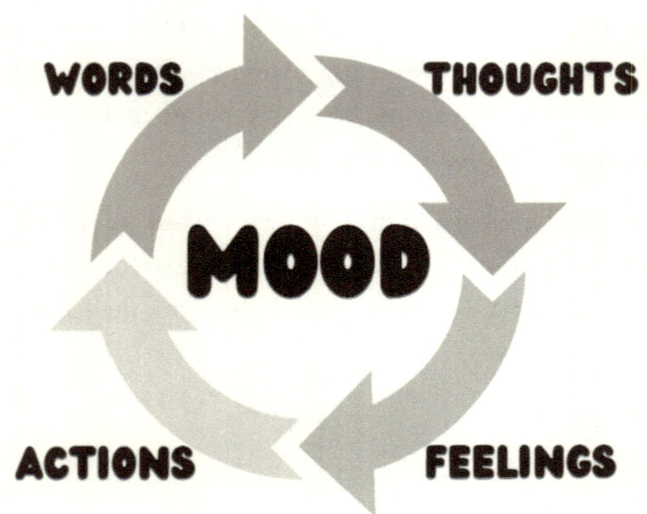

I'd like to introduce all of us to the mood loop. First of all, let's go over the definition of mood. Mood simply refers to how we feel at a particular time. Usually, people talk about being in a good mood or a bad mood. The major determinant of it is our words as it is the foundation where the mood loop begins at. I came up with it as a tool to bring about the quickest change possible in clients.

Our words lead to our thoughts and our thoughts lead to our feelings and our feelings determine our actions and the loop goes on and on accordingly. Now just practice the mood loop by constantly repeating some words like I am sad, I am sad, I am sad several times and just notice how it shifts your thinking and feelings and now try to get a sense of how it will show up in your actions.

On the contrary, try repeating words like I am happy, I am happy or all is well, all is well and notice how you think, feel and act and the overall difference between the two statements. Your mood can be lifted or dropped by using a few words.

Our words lead to similar thoughts and feelings that will further determine our actions. Our mood can also influence the mood loop of others as we all carry one and can immediately lift or drop others mood.

Just imagine for a couple of seconds a scenario if you tell someone, who cares about you that you had a really bad day today, what energy are your words emanating here and how it can affect the whole mood loop for the other person? On the other hand, if you say you had a good day or even better if you say your day was amazing today, just notice the difference it makes in their mood.

We can go and even test the second or the third scenario and see or feel how it positively affects their body language, words and their tonality. If you practice it, we'll see the mood loop live in action. Now we don't have to lie to improve someoone's mood but we can intentionally choose to use better high-energy words instead.

Just carefully select the words when we're communicating with our dear ones as we're now aware of how our words can impact their mood. And if we identify someone as an energy sucker at a particular moment whose mood loop is contradicting ours, we should go ahead and let them know that their words are affecting us and if we care about them at all then let them know that it's even affecting themselves as they'll be running in circles over and over again in their mood loop.

If someone ever comes back at us about what to do instead, then the ideal response would be to ask them to appreciate something in their lives or around at them. That'll immediately shift their energy and that will lead them to think and feel better. If they still don't want to be appreciative, wish them well.

When people start to notice wonderful changes in us, do share the mood loop with them so they can see how simple feeling good and pleasant can be if you plan on making it to be.

Our priority should always be our mood as we can't be in a bad mood and empower others and can't be in a good mood and disempower others. So let's be kind to ourselves and the dear ones around us.

Don't get caught in the mood loop of others and constantly choose your mood intentionally at the start of the day or even on a night before going to bed.

Choose that we'll primarily be in a good mood and use statements like I choose my mood, I have control over my mood to empower myself.

When our mood is being affected by someone, the antidote to that is what we've been learning so far in this book. Constantly use phrases like that's false, not for me, blah blah blah and take good care of ourselves .

It's ok to feel good and not so good at times as we go through our day-to-day lives but it's not ok to stay there for long and suffer as a result of it. More about this in the next chapter.

Q. What mood you'd like to choose to be primarily
in?

# CHAPTER 8

# THE EMOTIONAL GUIDANCE SCALE

| High Energy Activity |
|---|
| Joy / Appreciation / Empowered / Freedom / Love |
| Passion |
| Enthusiasm/ Eagerness / Happiness |
| Positive Expectation / Belief |
| Optimism |
| Hopefulness |
| Satisfaction / Contentment |

| Low Energy Activity |
|---|
| Boredom |
| Pessimisim |
| Frustration / Irritation / Impatience |
| Overwhelmed |
| Discouragement |
| Doubt |
| Worry |
| Blame |
| Discouragement |
| Anger |
| Revenge |
| Hatred/ Rage |
| Jealousy |
| Insecurity / Hurt / Guilt |
| Fear / Grief / Depression / Despair / Powerlessness |

From the book Ask & It Is Given. Jerry and Ester Hicks

The feelings arising from our mood will further define our emotions. Emotions are described as strong feelings that are derived from our mood.

There are two types of emotions - positive and negative ones, positive emotions denote high-energy activity and negative emotions denote low-energy activity. There are no in-betweens. So next time we say we're bored whether internally or out loud to someone, we're at the fine line where the low-energy activity or the negative emotions begin. Don't let the boredom turn into pessimism and further to frustration rather opt to go upwards towards the scale as that is where we can get more of what we want.

And how exactly to do that, that's what I am going to share next. I call it the appreciation game. Just appreciate five things about our lives to move up the scale and the next question could be what exactly to appreciate? Appreciate our presence on this planet, appreciate our eyes with which we are going through this book right now, appreciate the clothes you have on right now or a warm cup of our favourite drink. Just appreciate things, there is so much out there and the list can go on and on and on. Yes, that's how easy it is.

Or else we can play the blame and complain game and go down and down the scale and trust me, it's not fun down there. Whatever we focus on, expands. So the next time we catch ourselves feeling not so good or complaining about things, start appreciating things and shift our energy and emotions in seconds.

I'd request all of us to play this game right now as it'll take under a minute, we just need to appreciate 5 things and notice how our feelings shift immediately.

The major reason for sharing this scale is to show us the different layers of emotions and how it's more than just being happy or depressed as there's so much in between and how easy it is to change how we think, feel and experience different emotions on demand and no one has ever told us that this could be this easy.

Being aware of this scale will allow us to feel better than before and move up to a better emotion than we were experiencing before and make the most out of our moments of the day. Just repeating this game for a few days would be enough to make it automatic for us as we'll become appreciative in general and if we just look at the scale right now, appreciation sits at the top and the more we do it, the more fun it gets.

## Q. Which side of the emotional guidance scale would you like to be your dominating one?

# PERCEPTION IS PROJECTION

Perception refers to our sensory description of the world. We experience/ perceive the world through our 5 senses as discussed in Chapter 3 and they are visual (see), auditory (hear), kinesthetic (feel), olfactory (smell) and gustatory (taste) and we call them sub-modalities. Now let's close our eyes and think about 2 things one at a time first, a dish you like the most and notice its sub-modalities, what you see, hear, feel or check if you can even taste or smell them and then think about a dish you just hate and notice the difference in sub-modalities.

Now there's a difference in sub-modalities because of our perception about it. Either we have a positive perception about something or a negative one. If we have a positive perception about something doesn't mean that others can't have a negative perception about it and the same goes for the other way around.

For example - a friend we might have labelled as not a good one might be someone else's best friend. Now it's not our fault because they don't show up as someone who deserve the good friend tag in our life and might treat other individuals differently and they continue to show up in our life as they comply with our perception of them. Now it is mainly because of what we perceive about them through our 5 senses and we could have experienced it live or have heard about it.

So we have to shift our perception about something first to notice changes in the outside world or the world will continue to conform to our perception about them and prove to us right over and over again and just remember the phrase, SO BE IT.

Here I would like to share one of my favourite quotes -

> ***"The easier you can make it inside your head, the easier it will make things outside your head."***

**RICHARD BANDLER**

It's all about our perception of different things in our lives. We say something is hard or easy because the thing creates an image in our head and it is usually a giant-sized one for something we perceive as hard. All we have to do is make the image smaller in our head and perceive the things as doable because only when we shift our perception about it, we're opening up to the possibility of making it doable for us in life, just give it a try with something simple to start with like a vegetable, fruit etc. and experience it's all about our perception.

Just a quick example we all can relate with, back in the days of our school life when we used to dislike a particular subject or a teacher doesn't mean no one in our school found that subject easy or liked the teaching style of that particular teacher. So over the years, our perception hadn't shifted much or not at all about the subject or the teacher because we never knew we could shift our perception and we continued to believe it and it kept projecting in our lives.

So we have to intentionally choose to see good in most of the things every day because they are out there but we're just not focusing on them. Now if you ask me what is good to perceive right now in this very moment - The fact we have eyes to read this line.

I am going to share a quote with which we all can resonate with.

> *"Every day may not be good. But there's something good in every day."*
>
> **ALICE MORSE EARLE**

Now is the time to share my last metaphor to explain the concept of perception is projection and it's a fun one, I promise.

If we have a certain colour of glasses on, doesn't mean the world has changed its colour as it's only true for us. So we have to intentionally choose what glasses we'd like to put on and see different things in our lives. (Please refer to the following image.)

I'd like to finish this chapter with a fact - We can get spectacles for poor vision but what about our perspectives? (We got to do something about it ourselves)

**Q. What glasses are you going to choose for yourself from now on to look at different things in life?**

**Q. Can you spot a thing or two that does require a shift in your perception?**

# CHAPTER 10

# OVERCOME PAST MEMORIES

*I*f a kid regularly comes to our house and draws unusual stuff on the wall. What would we do most probably overtime? We'll repaint it. But what about the painful memories in our head, we keep them there for days, weeks, months and years unattended like they don't matter, but to be honest, it does. We can't keep them living rent-free in our heads as they can further lead to mental health issues. So let's learn how to get rid of them fast and effectively.

Because it could be the very reason why we can't enjoy moments of peace and happiness in our lives so far but not anymore. Now we're not going to delete them from our minds rather take the emotional intensity out of it so that whenever they come up in our day-to-day lives, we can smile at them and say that we don't care.

The next thing we're going to do is a simple three-minute exercise. We'll go with a recent unpleasant memory up to 3 - 6 months old to start with like something someone said to us about how we did something wrong, something we felt embarrassed about, a back and forth argument or something of that sort at work, school or at home that we just don't feel good about. so let's get started -

The exercise we're going to use here is called the photo crumbler. Kindly go through the steps of it first. This will be an eyes-closed exercise and chant FOCUS,FOCUS, FOCUS 10 times to bring our attention towards the here and now and then start with the step 1 of the exercise.

1. First of all, just picture the memory in your mind, you have to take an image of that memory or a part of it that was the most painful one and it is something you'd like to feel better about.
2. Notice where the photo of the memory is located in your mind, it could be on the left, centre or right side.
3. Next, you will take your writing hand and physically grab the photo like we would grab a photo out from an album.
4. Next, you'll start to crumble and crush it like a useless piece of paper and experience how that memory is losing its intensity as it is being crushed and crumbled like we don't care about it.
5. Now the last step, as you've crushed and crumbled the photo into small bits of paper and have taken

the intensity out of it. Just lift your hand with the crumbled pieces of the photo towards your mouth and blow air from your mouth and see the pieces fly away in the distance and notice they've flown so far in the distance that they're no longer visible. And open your eyes.

Just notice, how you're feeling right now, you might be feeling some sort of lightness, a burden lifted or you might be feeling something better. You can repeat this exercise multiple times to get rid of different memories as you'll get great at it over the time.

Now on the contrary, what about the positive experiences from our past? We as humans lose connection from all the pleasant memories fast and we can't let go of the negative ones and we hold on to them for long. Now we're going do another 3-minute fun exercise for our positive pleasant experiences which I call the photo amplifier exercise where I'd like you to think about a past pleasant memory like a celebration of some sort or a milestone event like graduation or simply the best appreciation or something of that sort. Once again, kindly go through the steps of the exercise first and then close your eyes and chant FOCUS, FOCUS, FOCUS 10 times to bring your attention towards the here and now and then start with the step 1 of the exercise.

1. First of all, picture the pleasant memory in your mind, so you have to take a photo of that memory or a part of it that was the most pleasant one and you'd like to feel great about it again.
2. Notice where the photo of the memory is located in your mind, it could be on the left, centre or right side.
3. Next, you will take your writing hand and physically grab the photo like you would grab a photo out from an album.
4. Next, you'll push the photo back towards the biggest movie screen you've ever seen and see the memory on the movie screen and amplify the feelings of it as if it's happening right now.
5. You can even see yourself as being a part of the movie playing on the screen and see what you saw, hear what you heard and feel how good it felt as if it's happening right now.

I'm sure you had a wonderful experience and you know what's the best part about it, you can use it for several pleasant experiences from your life and feel good on demand and that's a priceless skill to possess in today's world where mental issues are at an all-time high. So let's make our pleasant memories stronger and get rid of the unpleasant ones.

Doing this exercise multiple times a day and making it automatic will ultimately help us shift our words, we will think good as a result of it and it will impact how great we feel and we'd be able to notice it in our actions.

And when our actions are on point, it'll impact our emotions and we will be on the high energy level of the scale throughout the day and we'll automatically perceive the best in almost all the situations. And we will enjoy moments of peace and happiness in our life and that's the primary reason why we're going through this book.

We're almost done with mastering the skill of how to make the most out of the currency of our lives and we now know how to spend it well as we'll be spending it more in doing what we want in our life. Now is the time for the next chapter where I will share how easy it is to change limiting beliefs and create new empowering ones as it is another important skill worth possessing.

**Q. Do you plan on using the exercises shared in this chapter intentionally to create moments of instant peace and happiness in your life?**

# CHAPTER 11

# CHANGING BELIEFS MADE SIMPLE YET EFFECTIVE

*A* belief is a repeated thought you have in your mind, an acceptance that something is true and one has confidence and trust in it. For eg. if one is not good at math and has constantly heard and spoken out loud in the world that math is hard, math is hard. Guess what, it's a deep-rooted belief now and it will be true for you until you plan to do something about it.

Beliefs do work like this, believe it to see it and not what the majority of the world thinks that they'll believe something only when they see it, that's going backwards. Let me share some examples about it. A beautiful monument was planned first in terms of how it'd look like and then it's later turned into a reality. Any great invention was first just a belief to create something and then it changed into reality, a seed was planted with an expectation of a shady tree from it and the same goes for our lives as our beliefs act as self-imposed hurdles. I'm sure, you have grasped the idea of believing it first to see it and how beliefs work in our lives.

They are relatively easy to spot and could be like I am lazy, I am not good enough, I am ugly, I could do that but I am not good at it or something you repeatedly say to yourself and believe fully in it. I'll share 3 quick yet effective methods to overcome such limiting beliefs and create new empowering ones.

The first method is our 6th phrase where you will intentionally call upon the limiting belief and say the belief to be changed internally and just after you've finished the sentence, answer it with -

## JUST A THOUGHT

Repeat it around 10 times intentionally for a couple of days and you'll start to believe it as just a thought and changing our thoughts is as easy as changing our socks. So what we're doing here is turning a belief into a thought so that we'll perceive it in a new way. Just try bringing up the limiting belief and reply to it with just a thought multiple times and notice how your thinking and feelings shift.

The second method is the written one which involves us declaring with our written words and it goes like this -

Up until now, it was the case that I couldn't ........ and now I claim my ability to .......... in every way!

That's how easy the written method is, just write down these 2 lines and include your beliefs in it to notice the change in how you feel. Now is the time for the third and my favourite method – true and false. Just bring up an image in your mind of something true and say to yourself My name is ..... (your name) and notice where is it located, how it sounds like and how good you feel when you hear your name.

On the contrary, you should say another statement like My name is ...... (not your name) and see its image and how low quality it is, notice your sound, how doubtful you sound as there's something false about it, feel how you feel when someone calls you with a false name and open your eyes. Notice the difference between the two and now you can again close your eyes and have the limiting belief attached to the false statement like My name is .... (not your name) and I am ..... (limiting belief) and repeat the statement 5 times internally.

On the other hand, attach your new empowering belief to your name like My name is .... (your real name) and I am ... (new empowering belief) and repeat the statement 5 times internally. And notice how great it feels when you can start to feel the truth of the new empowering belief. Repeat it 3 times a day for a week and notice the wonderful shifts you make.

So that sums up the last chapter of the book but wait, where's the 7th phrase? You'll learn about it in the next section, before that I want to make sure that you've gone through all the exercises and phrases mentioned in the chapters above.

# *Epilogue*

$I$'m really glad you've made it to this point. I know you're waiting for the 7th phrase, the 7th phrase is –

## SAY AND SEE WHAT YOU WANT

I can't emphasise enough how powerful it is. The world has programmed us to see what could go wrong and I have a question for all of us to answer instead, what if it goes right, how great it would be? Can we all just take some time and imagine how it'd be if we programmed ourselves to say and see what we want?

What's great about this is we train our mind to know what we want more of as it has already learned the patterns of worry, anger and whatnot by constantly reminding it of what worry and anger look like and it became automatic for us. Even if we say and see what we don't want, we have empowered ourselves to use the 7 phrases and tell our mind what we do want instead.

Go out and try using the phrases from now on and head in the direction you'd like to go in and accept nothing costing us our peace and happiness. Mix and match them, use the 2 gestures to shield and protect yourself as well and see what combination works the best for you. To be honest with you, no one is stopping you from making it a reality for you, only you are. Suffering is a choice and in the same way, empowerment is a choice as well and as you're reading this line, I can hear a loud empowerment coming my way.

> ***"Life is really simple but we insist on making it complicated."***

> **CONFUCIUS**

We can't control several things in our lives but certainly, we can have a strong influence over our words, how we react to others words, our moods, emotions, perceptions, and what memories we would like to get rid of and which ones to amplify. Embrace the learnings from the book and the world and most importantly you will soon notice a change in how you're reacting to different things in life. Go through this book at least twice or thrice as every time you'll notice something that you may have missed the first time.

> ***"The book remains the same, but the reader changes and grows every time."***

I trust you'll make the best use of the information you've gained from the book. Until next time, take good care of yourself and keep smiling, Ciao!

# Review Time

- Our words have energy
- The 3 types of talks we have in our lives
- The 3 broad categories of people in our lives
- So Be It
- Cancel, cancel, cancel
- That's false
- Not for me
- Blah, blah, blah
- Just a thought
- The mood loop
- Emotional guidance scale
- Perception is projection
- The photo crumble and the photo amplifier exercise
- The true and false exercise
- Say and see what you want

# About The Author

*J*apjot Kang is a smile generator and a hope creator. He's a business graduate turned into a Neuro-Linguistic Programming Master Practitioner, a emotional and mental wellness coach and a Amazon Bestselling Author. He loves to help people struggling in managing their emotions make simple yet lasting changes in their lives. His mission in life is to reduce suffering, empower others and make this planet a wonderful place to live in. If you have a query or you want to know about his DFY online coaching services and online courses, you can reach out to him via Email. hello@japjotkang.com